Princess Poppy

The Unicorn Foal

www.**randomhousechildrens**.co.uk

*Check out Princess Poppy's website
to find out all about the other
books in the series*
www.princesspoppy.com

Princess Poppy

The Unicorn Foal

written by Janey Louise Jones
Illustrated by Samantha Chaffey

THE UNICORN FOAL
A YOUNG CORGI BOOK 978 0 552 57146 3

Published in Great Britain by Young Corgi,
an imprint of Random House Children's Publishers UK
A Penguin Random House Company

Penguin
Random House
UK

This edition published 2015

3 5 7 9 10 8 6 4 2

Penguin Random House is committed to a sustainable future for
our business, our readers and our planet. This book is made from
Forest Stewardship Council® certified paper.

MIX
Paper from
responsible sources
FSC® C018179
www.fsc.org

Young Corgi Books are published by Random House Children's Publishers UK,
61–63 Uxbridge Road, London W5 5SA

www.randomhousechildrens.com
www.totallyrandombooks.co.uk
www.randomhouse.co.uk

Addresses for companies within The Random House Group Limited
can be found at: www.randomhouse.co.uk/offices.htm

THE RANDOM HOUSE GROUP Limited Reg. No. 954009

A CIP catalogue record for this book is available from the British Library.

Printed in Great Britain by Clays Ltd, St Ives plc

For Ana Afonso and her daughter, Princesa Joana.

Chapter One

Poppy was very glad that school was over for another year. She had been looking forward to the summer holidays for *ages*. It was the first day of the break – a bright sunny morning – and before she got out of bed, she looked at her checklist of everything she wanted to do that summer.

Summer Holiday to Do List – Poppy Cotton (Princess)

1. <u>Perfect Cartwheels</u>
2. Write to my pen pal
3. Try out a ballet bun – <u>decorate with freshly picked rosebuds</u>
4. Help Mum more around the house (maybe if bored)
5. Paint Twinkletoe's <u>stable door with glitter paint</u>
6. <u>Grow my nails</u>
7. Make a perfect strawberry Pavlova with Granny Bumble
8. Help Grandpa with his vegetables for Country Show
9. Read favourite fairy tales (write better endings for them)
10. <u>Clothes shopping at Re-Bloom Boutique</u>

Mum popped her head round the door. "Poppy!" she said. "Honey will be leaving soon. You should go and say goodbye."

"Really? Already?" said Poppy, her heart sinking. Was it really today that Honey was leaving for her big fancy cruise? *I don't want her to go away!* she thought.

"Yes, her mum and dad arrived at Honeypot Cottage last night and they're busy packing. Granny Bumble just popped over to borrow one of your swimsuits for Honey," said Mum. "I gave her the lilac one – it was on the line, and I knew you wouldn't mind."

"No, I don't mind at all," Poppy replied.

"Don't look so glum, sweetheart," said Mum. "You've known for a while that Honey was going away at the start of the holidays. She hardly ever gets to see her parents, so it's nice for her."

"I know, I know," said Poppy. "I had just forgotten, that's all."

She glanced at her checklist again. She felt so flat. There was nothing properly exciting on it. Nothing inspiring. Nothing adventurous. *What I'd really like is a big adventure,* she decided.

After waving goodbye to Honey, Poppy was very restless; she didn't feel like doing anything. She looked at her list.

She did a cartwheel. That took twenty seconds. She tried to write to her Dutch pen pal, Klara, who she'd met on holiday in Portugal, but after saying,

How are you? she lost interest. Then she sat at her dressing table and tried out different ballet buns. But none of them looked right. It was as if even her hair was in a bad mood! She ignored the 'help  Mum around the house' idea, as she didn't want to send herself completely crazy with boredom.

Painting Twinkletoes' stable door was definitely a nice idea, but Grandpa's sister, Aunt Marigold, who ran the General Store in Honeypot Hill, had ordered glitter paint and had promised to call when it arrived. So far, there had been no call. Everything else on the list sounded far too unadventurous.

Poppy decided that the only thing of any interest at all was clothes shopping at the Re-Bloom Boutique.

A new family had recently opened the store and it was a wonderful treasure trove of pretty things: skirts and tops, fancy dresses, shoes and bags, jewellery and scarves. There were also beautiful paintings, curious black-and-white photographs, antique pieces of furniture, and quirky things like old-fashioned telephones and radios, which always made

Poppy think of the people who had first owned them, and how they had lived their lives.

Yes, that's what I'll do, she decided, suddenly feeling positive again. *I will go down to the village and visit the Blooms. Perhaps Violet Bloom will be in the shop. She's so incredibly cool! I wish I was a teenager like Violet.*

Poppy decided to change so she'd look her best down in the village. She co-ordinated her outfit carefully: a white skirt, a blue top with white butterflies, and her favourite white espadrilles. She brushed her hair carefully and caught it back behind her ears with her favourite poppy hair clips. Just a dab of the petal perfume Honey had made for her, and she was almost ready to go.

Finally she brushed her teeth, found her handbag and took some pennies out of

her piggy-bank, then raced down to the
Re-Bloom Boutique, calling goodbye as
she went.

The window of the boutique was as
lovely as ever, with a stripy deckchair in
the centre, along with antique buckets
and spades, as well as a very old sign
for ice-cream cones. *Oooh, it's a holiday-
themed window! That's nice!* thought Poppy.
She gazed at the interesting display, with
embroidered silk shawls and fancy parasols
and lots of old-fashioned postcards – the
sort that people used to post from their
holidays years ago.

Poppy imagined herself as a Victorian
girl, with a pretty, frilly white dress and
a straw hat, sitting on a beach, writing
postcards . . . *Hello, Honey. Wish we were on
holiday together . . .*

The shop bell rang as Poppy stepped
inside.

Chapter 2

Inside the boutique, Violet Bloom was pulling a watermelon-pink prom dress over the head of a mannequin.

"Hi, Violet!" said Poppy, with a broad smile.

"Hey – you're Poppy, right?"

"Yes, that's right. Is it OK if I have a browse around?"

"Sure." Violet gave her a flicker of a smile.

Poppy looked at the rails of children's

clothes, glancing over at Violet from time to time. *She looks so pretty!* she thought. *I love her dress. How does she get her hair to look like that? I wish I was allowed to wear make-up.*

Poppy tried on a wide-brimmed straw hat and peered in the mirror.

"Looks great," said Violet.

"Do you think so?" Poppy was thrilled by the compliment.

Just then the shop door burst open and Violet's brother, Jonny Bloom, breezed in. "Oh, hi, Poppy!" he said. "Nice hat!"

"Hi!" said Poppy, removing the hat and trying another. "What've you been up to?"

"Not much. I thought the holidays would be great," said Jonny, "but I'm actually bored already!"

"Snap!" said Poppy. "Maybe we could set up a club, or do a project or something?"

"Well, I'm going away with my family

next week," said Jonny. "In our camper van!"

At this, Violet turned round and rolled her eyes. "Worst luck!"

"But that sounds like great fun," said Poppy. "I wish we were doing something like that. Where are you going?"

"It's this place called Fairy Moon," said

Jonny. "We've been before. My mum keeps saying that it's where fairies live, but I've never seen any."

"Oooh, *Fairy Moon*!" said Poppy. "That sounds amazing!"

"It's really cool. Where are you going for your holiday?" asked Jonny.

"Nowhere this year," she said. "Mum and Dad have spent too much money already. Or maybe I have – I'm not exactly sure!"

"Maybe you could all come to Fairy Moon too. My mum says it doesn't cost much. We're really hard up as well, because we've spent lots on this shop and all the stock . . ."

"It sounds awesome," said Poppy. "But my mum hates sleeping in a tent and we don't have a camper van."

"Hmmm. That *is* a problem," said Jonny. "Why don't we go for a wander around

the village? I bet *someone* has a spare
camper van!"

"Cool!" exclaimed Poppy, and she
and Jonny stepped out into the hot sun
and strolled along the banks of the River
Swan.

"Let's ask Aunt Marigold if she
knows of anyone with a camper van,"
she suggested. As Aunt Marigold ran
the General Store, she tended to hear
everything.

But Aunt Marigold said that, no,

unfortunately she did not know of anyone
with a camper van.

"Oh, Lily Ann Peach at the Beauty
Salon knows *everyone* in the village – I'll
see what she says," said Poppy.

They ambled cheerfully along the street.
Soon they arrived outside the Beauty Salon.

"Erm, I'm not coming in there!" said
Jonny. "It stinks of perfume and shampoo
and stuff!"

"OK, you wait here," said Poppy with a
giggle as she went into the salon.

"Hi, Poppy," said Lily Ann. "Don't you look lovely today! How can I help you?"

"Do you know of anyone who has a camper van or caravan?" asked Poppy.

Lily Ann shook her head. "Sorry, love," she said. "Years ago, lots of people had caravans and holiday vans, but . . ." Lily Ann was distracted as one of her clients popped her head out from under a noisy overhead dryer.

"Did she say 'camper van'?" asked the lady; she looked a bit like an alien, with lines of neatly attached rollers all over her head.

The face was very familiar to Poppy, though. The sweet-faced, plump alien with the *Knitting Monthly* magazine on her lap was someone she knew very well.

"Hey, is that you, Mrs Meadowsweet?" she asked.

"Yes, of course it's me, love!" said Mrs Meadowsweet. "You think my hair gets to be so beautiful all by itself?"

Poppy giggled. She didn't think Mrs Meadowsweet's hair was *ever* exactly beautiful, but that was just because she liked long hair better than short, bubbly styles.

"That's a lot of rollers!" she said.

"Did you say you were looking for a camper van?" asked Mrs Meadowsweet.

"Yes – it's just that we haven't got a holiday planned this year and the Blooms are going to this gorgeous place called Fairy Moon, and I thought . . ." Poppy trailed off sadly.

Mrs Meadowsweet and Lily Ann shared a look.

"You do an *awful* lot of thinking,

Princess Poppy Cotton," said Mrs Meadowsweet. "The thing is, we do have an old camper van in the barn. Farmer Meadowsweet uses it to sleep in during the lambing season if he has to stay out at night on the hill. But it's in a horrible, filthy state. It really is in need of attention! And your parents deserve a good rest, not extra cleaning jobs!"

"But I could fix it up!" said Poppy excitedly. "I'm good at jobs like that!"

"Well you'd have to see what your mum says first," said Mrs Meadowsweet. "You're more than welcome to it if she agrees."

Before another word could be uttered, Poppy had said her goodbyes and bounded out into the street, where she almost knocked Jonny down in her excitement.

"Come on – we've got to go and speak

to my mum!" she cried. "I think I've found us a camper van!"

"Yahooo!" said Jonny. "I *knew* we'd find one!"

Chapter 3

Mum was in the garden of Honeysuckle Cottage, finishing a big wedding hat for the mother of a bride.

"Hello, you two!" she said. "What've you been up to?"

"Oh, Mum! We've had this great idea!" said Poppy breathlessly.

"Oh dear," said Mum nervously. "What's that, Poppy?"

"Well," she began, "you know how we can't afford a holiday and everyone else in

the whole wide world is going on holiday
apart from us . . . ? The thing is, Jonny
and his family are going to this campsite
called Fairy Moon – it's enchanted by
fairies – in their camper van, and it
doesn't cost much. So I thought, maybe we
could go——"

"Oh, Poppy, hang on a minute. You know how much I hate tents – and how would we get a camper van?" Mum was now hanging up the washing – pegging out a lovely little smock dress that had once been Poppy's but now belonged to Angel.

"That's the whole point. I've already found us one!"

Mum stopped what she was doing. "Poppy, you go out for half an hour and come back with a full holiday plan!" she said. "How can you just *find* a camper van?"

"It's Farmer Meadowsweet's – he sleeps in it during lambing, but Mrs Meadowsweet says we can have it if we like. We'd just need to clean it up . . ." explained Poppy.

"Oh, I see . . . And when are you going to Fairy Moon, Jonny?" Mum asked.

"Next week," he replied. "It would be awesome if you came because Violet is no fun on holiday – or ever, actually – and I'd love it if Poppy was there. It would be an adventure."

"Mum, you KNOW I love adventures!" said Poppy. "Pleeease."

Mum seemed to be thinking hard. "This is all a bit sudden . . . Let me think about it while I do some sewing jobs this afternoon."

"OK . . ." Poppy found it so frustrating the way adults always thought about things for absolutely ages, worrying about what if *this* happened, or *that* happened. And after all that thinking, and chatting on the telephone, and writing down notes, and looking at stuff on the internet, you could never quite tell whether they would say yes or no! *Really, they should just DO things and then think afterwards*, decided

Poppy. *That's what I do.*

She turned to Jonny. "Let's go down to Barley Farm and see if we can find the van," she whispered. "And we can say hello to Twinkletoes while we're there!"

"Sure!" said Jonny. "You don't waste any time, Poppy!"

"Grandpa always says, 'There's no time like the present!' I'll take my camera, because I know Mum will ask, 'So what's this camper van like?' and it will be good if I can show her some pictures! And I can e-mail some to Honey too."

Poppy gathered what she needed in her backpack. Mum was sitting in the rocking chair, darning socks and sewing buttons back onto cardigans, which she often did during the twins' nap times.

"Bye, Mum!" Poppy called.

"Oh, where are you going now?" asked Mum.

"Just to the stables."

"OK – don't be late for tea. Jonny can come too, if he likes . . ."

"OK, thanks. Bye!" chimed Poppy and Jonny.

And they ran all the way to Barley Farm.

Chapter 4

"Come and meet Twinkletoes!" cried
Poppy, rushing over to her pony's loose
box. She undid the door and ran over
to hug him. The little pony nuzzled her
contentedly.

Jonny patted his neck. "Why's he called
Twinkletoes?" he asked.

"Because he has twinkly white feet –
look!"

"So he does!" said Jonny. "He's lovely!"

"He's the best," said Poppy. "I could

play with him all day. But we've got to
find this van!"

She bolted the stable door, saying,
"Bye-bye, Twinks. I'll be back soon! And
don't forget, you'll have a glittery door by
the end of the summer!"

Poppy knew her way around Barley
Farm very well and she led Jonny towards
the barn. A big green sliding door was
very slightly ajar. "Let's go in and take a
look," she said.

The door was stiff, but they managed
to slide it open, little by little, until the gap
was big enough for them to slip through.

It was dark inside the barn and it smelled of grass. Poppy reached into her backpack. "I brought a torch!" she announced.

"Wow! You've thought of everything!" said Jonny. "Now let's try and work out where the camper van is."

It was a huge barn. Poppy followed Jonny, but they couldn't see much, and wandered around aimlessly. Poppy began to think they'd never find the van, but then Jonny called out, "Over here!"

There, in front of them, was a very old camper van. It looked a bit like the Blooms' one, but it was completely filthy.

"Oh my goodness!" Poppy exclaimed. "It certainly does need a good clean!"

It was impossible to even say what colour the van was. It was covered in dirt and dust and straw and cobwebs.

Nervously Poppy opened the driver's door and peered inside. "Euuughh! It smells absolutely awful! I think the sheep must live in here," she said. "Do you really think five of us could sleep in this?" For the first time she sounded as if she thought perhaps it wasn't the best idea after all.

"I think it will be fine after a good clean," said Jonny encouragingly. "And you could take a tent for you or your dad to sleep in if it's too squashed – we have a spare one we can lend you. It's great fun, sleeping outdoors – with no nagging about routines and tidying rooms and stuff. We can spend our time gathering driftwood, building fires, singing songs and toasting marshmallows. Come on, Poppy, the van isn't *that* bad. There might be some curtains and cushions in the boutique that we can use to make it really nice . . ."

Jonny was quite convincing. Poppy just

knew that if Mum saw the van as it was, in this terrible state, she'd say that it was too horrid and Poppy should forget the whole idea of a holiday this year.

"I think we'll have to clean it up and make it pretty before my mum sees it," she said. "And I definitely won't be showing her the 'before' photos!"

"I can help," Jonny offered.

"We'll have to ask Farmer Meadowsweet if it's OK first," said Poppy. "He got a bit annoyed with me when I didn't turn up on time to clean his cart for the Royal Parade. I just hope he trusts me enough . . ."

"But did you get the cart cleaned in the end?" asked Jonny.

"Oh, yes, it was sparkling for the parade."

"Well, then he knows you can do it. I'm sure it'll be fine. Let's go and find him!"

Farmer Meadowsweet was grading

potatoes in the potato shed near his fallow field.

"Before you ask, if it's about the camper van, help yourself. Mrs Meadowsweet has already sorted it out," he said. "Sorts out the whole world down in that Beauty Salon."

"Wow, really?" Poppy beamed from ear to ear. "So you don't mind if we clean it up?"

"Mind? Why would I mind? I'd have to pay a fortune to get that thing cleaned. Go and see Mrs Meadowsweet, and she'll give you cloths and buckets and sprays and what-not. No point in carrying all that down from the village!"

"Oh, thank you!" cried Poppy. "Maybe we *will* get a holiday after all!"

She skipped across to the farmhouse with Jonny at her side. They collected the cleaning stuff and headed back to the barn.

Farmer Meadowsweet drove the van out into the courtyard and parked it right by the tap and hose.

"Cleaning this van could be the start of my great summer adventure!" said Poppy. Farmer Meadowsweet helped take some photographs for Poppy to send to Honey!

First they hosed the van down, until all the loose dirt and dust had been washed off. Then they fetched warm water from the farmhouse and mixed it with soap to make bubbles.

Jonny gave himself a beard of white bubbles and said: "Ho ho ho! What would you like for Christmas?" which made Poppy giggle.

They washed the van thoroughly and then hosed off the bubbles. Soon it was gleaming.

"Phew, that's enough work for one day!" said Poppy. "We can tackle the

inside tomorrow. Let's take one more picture of the outside so I can send Honey a 'before and after'. She'll be amazed!"

Under all the dirt and dust the van was pink and white, and it really did sparkle after the big clean.

When Poppy got home, she showed Mum the picture of the *clean* van.

"Oh, it's not bad at all." Mum sounded quite enthusiastic. "I'd better call the Meadowsweets and the Blooms and this Fairy Moon place, to explore the idea a bit further . . ."

Poppy felt very excited as she played with the twins to keep them quiet, while Mum chatted on the phone for a very long time.

That night, at tea time, the conversation turned to the camper van.

"James," said Mum as Dad sat down for tea, "Poppy's come up with an idea . . ."

"Oh dear. Is it going to be *very* expensive?" asked Dad, with a smile.

"No – you see, the Blooms have a camper van and they're going to a campsite called Fairy Moon . . . well, I've spoken to Rose Bloom and she says we could join them . . ."

"Only we don't have a camper van or a tent . . ." Dad pointed out.

"Ta-da!" Poppy produced her camera and showed him the picture of the cleaned-up camper van. "Farmer Meadowsweet says we can borrow this, and Jonny and I have cleaned it out!" she told him excitedly.

"Tell me more," said Dad.

Poppy described what had happened and then listened carefully as Mum and Dad talked non-stop about insurance and supplies and fuel costs and Dad getting time off work, and so many other boring things that she almost lost concentration.

"So can we go or not?" she asked
finally.

"We'll tell you in the morning," said
Dad. "But it's a lovely idea, darling. Thank
you!"

That did not sound too hopeful, Poppy
thought. *Nice idea, but not this year, Poppy,*
she imagined them saying.

She asked Mum to help her send
pictures of the camper van to Honey. And
when they looked at her e-mails, they saw
that Honey had sent her some pictures
too.

"Wow!" said Poppy as she looked at the
images of a sunny Greek Island. "I don't
think my pictures are going to be as cool
as Honey's."

"Don't be silly – doing up a camper van is really great fun," said Mum. "Why don't you go and read in your room so Dad and I can discuss it?"

Poppy tossed and turned all night. It seemed as if the whole summer was stretching out endlessly ahead of her, and she really wanted to go on this adventure. *I'll be so sad when Jonny goes away – and Honey will still be in Greece!* she thought. *Oh, please let them say we can go . . .*

Chapter 5

The next morning Poppy went down for breakfast feeling nervous. She'd already done more than half the things on her checklist. A summer without going away was going to be horrid.

"Well, have you decided?" she asked.

Mum and Dad looked at her.

"We're going!" cried Mum. "Oh, well done, Poppy! It's a lovely idea – I don't really fancy not going away either."

So it was decided. Poppy was going

to have a holiday after all. Time to tell
Jonny!

She quickly got dressed and dashed over
to the Blooms'. She rang the bell excitedly
and Jonny came to the door.

She didn't have to say a word – her grin
said it all.

"Cooool!" he said. "Fairy Moon, here
we come!"

Farmer Meadowsweet drove the camper
van up to Honeysuckle Cottage, and
Poppy and Mum set about finishing off
the cleaning and decoration.

"Decorating is possibly my best skill!"
said Poppy. "I can't wait to make the
inside look beautiful!"

They swept it out, then cleaned and
polished every corner until everything
gleamed. They draped bits of material
from the Blooms' boutique at the
windows, and Poppy finished it off by

adding stickers of poppies to the outside.

"Now it looks fabulous!" she said. "I'll send Honey a picture of the inside!"

It was nearly time to set off for Fairy Moon, and Poppy was helping Mum and Dad pack the van with clothes, towels, bedding, food, games and wash things.

Jonny came over to see how they were getting on. "We're all packed. My mum's going crazy at Violet, though. She has done NOTHING to help and says she wants to stay at home. But Mum says

44

there's no way she's going to stay home alone, so we're stuck with her being a pain! She usually just ignores me. Do you want to travel in our van, Poppy, so I've got someone to talk to?" he wondered.

"Sure," said Poppy. "That will be really cool, 'cos the twins are a bit annoying as well – in a different way – they say a bit too much!"

Dad drove over to the Blooms', where Poppy jumped out and climbed up into Jonny's van.

"See you there,"
called Mum.

"OK, cool," said
Poppy.

She listened to
the mums and dads
chatting about the
route and fuel and
timings. *Why don't
they just get on with it?
Boring!* she thought.

"Hi, Violet!" said Poppy as she settled
into her seat in the Blooms' van.

Violet had her earphones in and didn't
reply.

"Violet, don't be rude – Poppy said
'Hi'," said her mother, Rose, gently taking
the earphones out.

"What? Oh yeah – hey," said Violet,
promptly putting them back in again.

"Ignore her," said Jonny. "Look, I've

started a scrap book all about our trip –
I've written down the route and stuff."

Poppy was so impressed with his
adventure book. "Wow, that's cool," she
said. "I keep a scrap book too." She and
Jonny got on so well – they liked doing
lots of the same things.

Poppy glanced at Violet; she wondered
what it would be like to be fourteen and
beautiful, and so cool that you didn't want

to please anyone. She gazed out of the window, and with every field they passed, the countryside became just a little more magical. The grass got greener, the sky bluer and the trees prettier. The sun shone down brightly and covered the landscape in golden light. *We must be near Fairy Moon,* Poppy thought, *because I can just imagine fairies dancing in these trees.*

She was bursting with excitement by the time the entrance sign for the Fairy Moon campsite came into sight.

WELCOME TO
FAIRY MOON
Where Holiday Dreams
Come True

Chapter 6

The lady at the office showed them a
site map marked with a star where they
should set up camp, at the edge of the
meadow.

As they drove in, Poppy gasped. "It's so
beautiful!" she breathed.

The trees round the edges of the
meadow seemed to be in conversation
with each other, while the dappled
sunshine played on the blowing grasses.
The wild flowers – poppies, daisies and

cornflowers – shimmered like precious
rubies, diamonds and sapphires.

"I really *can* imagine fairies living here,"
said Poppy. "And I'm quite sure they make
dresses from petals, and houses from twigs
and leaves!"

Honey would love this, she thought. She
took out her camera and snapped away,
then turned to see if Violet was equally
excited. But Violet was still listening to
music, her eyes shut.

I wonder why she doesn't even look at this

lovely place! thought Poppy.

Once they had parked, Poppy and Jonny jumped out of the van and gazed across the beautiful sunlit meadow. There were tents and camper vans and caravans dotted here, there and everywhere. Sheep grazed in the distance, chickens pecked nosily around the campers, and Poppy caught sight of a squirrel scampering up a tree, and then –

"Oh, look!" she cried. "A peacock! It's so colourful!"

Best of all, at the edge of the site she saw some ponies – ten of them, mostly munching grass or basking in the sunshine. But a little white mare was prancing anxiously around the field. *Gosh, she's so elegant*, thought Poppy.

She was distracted by Jonny, who couldn't wait to show her around and start setting up camp.

"Shall Poppy and I go and collect kindling – and water from the river?" he suggested; he had been through this routine before.

"Great idea!" said Rose. "Here's a basket and a pail. Be careful, though! And you know the rules – don't cross the river."

"Yeah, Mum, don't worry," said Jonny. "This way, Poppy . . ." He led her through a clearing in the trees, along a shady path towards the river. Poppy could hear water tinkling over pebbles, and soon the river emerged, bright and magical. The sun bounced off it here and there, making it look like a stream of liquid gold.

Suddenly, ahead of her, Poppy saw stepping stones that led across to the other side. Bathed in sunlit water, the stones were tempting nuggets of gold.

"Shall we see what's across the river?" she whispered. *I'm sure that's where the fairies live*, she thought.

"No!" said Jonny. "We're not allowed. We should just get the kindling and water. Maybe the adults will take us exploring later. I'd like to show you the den I made with a boy I met here last year. It's further along this side of the river."

"Cool," said Poppy. "Now, tell me what kind of kindling to look for . . ."

Jonny pointed to bits of driftwood, twigs and sticks. "Anything like that," he said. "We can dry them in the sun and use

them to start our campfire. I love it after
dark here. We can toast marshmallows and
tell stories till late. We *used* to do all that,
anyway, although the last couple of times
we've been here, Violet has been moody
and mean and ruined it for everyone."

"It's a shame she's like that," said Poppy
as she gathered twigs and sticks and threw
them into the basket. "I'd really like to get
to know her better. She's cool."

"She used to be fun and really kind,"
said Jonny. "But she's changed. My mum

says she's going to ban all technology if
Violet doesn't read a book and chat to us
this holiday. But Mum will never actually
do that – Violet is even more annoying
without her phone!"

Once they'd gathered enough wood
to get a fire going, and Jonny had filled
the pail with water, they headed along
the path towards the meadow again.
Poppy looked back over her shoulder at
the golden stepping stones. *There must be
some good reason for crossing to the other side,*

she decided. *Otherwise, why would there be stepping stones?* She thought she heard fairies singing in the distance.

As soon as the tents were pitched, it was time for supper. Poppy helped Jonny's father, Ralph, to cook fried potatoes with sweet shallots, slices of smoked bacon and beans. It was getting dusky, and although the air was cool, Poppy didn't feel cold because the campfire was blazing and Rose had set out lanterns with candles. It looked cosy and enchanted, like the scene

of a fairy feast. Jonny and his dad played their banjos, and everyone sang "Head, Shoulders, Knees and Toes!"

Mum and Dad looked so relaxed and happy, Poppy thought. The twins fell asleep and the stars twinkled down on them. At that moment, she believed in magic more than ever.

"Is it true that fairies live in this glade?" she asked, turning to Rose.

"Well, there have been lots of sightings," she replied. "And one year I spoke to an old lady who'd been coming here since she was a child, and she said she once saw a unicorn on the other side of the river!"

"Wow!" gasped Poppy. "I LOVE unicorns!"

Violet tutted from the other side of the fire. "Honestly, Mum, you'll believe anything! It's so embarrassing!"

"Well, you have to believe in magic to

experience it," said Rose. "So, bad luck, Vi
– you'll never see anything extraordinary."

"I hate family holidays!" said Violet
huffily. "I hate Fairy Moon."

"Don't go spreading your negative thoughts around!" said Ralph. "We're having a lovely time!"

"You are all PATHETIC!" said Violet, flouncing off, with her mum and dad following crossly.

Poppy was shocked. Mum and Dad exchanged glances which she thought said something like: *Thank goodness we don't have one of those teenager people yet.*

That night, Poppy dreamed that across the river fairies were dancing with a unicorn; they were laughing and saying: "*Some humans don't believe we're real . . . silly billies . . .*"

Chapter 7

The following morning Poppy jumped up
the minute her eyes opened.

Breakfast was scrumptious. Mum and
Dad made a huge pot of creamy porridge,
using milk from the farm shop, laced with
blueberries and swirled with fresh blossom
honey. Afterwards Poppy went for a wander
on her own, with her camera. She decided
to look for wild flowers, and sat at the
edge of the meadow, near the ponies' field,
lost in her daydreams, weaving together

the stems of poppies, cornflowers and daisies. *This is a proper fairy crown*, she thought as she admired it.

Poppy placed the floral circlet on her head and watched the ponies. Most were grazing contentedly – but the white mare still looked agitated. *I think she's just dancing*, Poppy decided, but she was not completely sure she was right about that.

She got up and wandered along the tree-line, knowing that the intriguing golden river flowed just beyond the woods. What had Rose said last night? That you have to believe in magic to experience it? Poppy believed, that was for sure. *So why don't I experience it?* she wondered impatiently. Poppy was forever getting told off for being impatient, and she tried not to be, but sometimes it was impossible to wait! *Meeting a fairy or a unicorn would be wonderful*, she thought. *The sooner the better.*

She ambled back to the campsite. The first thing she noticed was that Violet was wearing very cool floral shorts and a pretty sun-top. The second thing she noticed was that Violet was scowling.

"Oh, nice crown!" said Rose. "You look lovely. Like a fairy princess!"

Poppy beamed at that.

"Anyone fancy coming for a ramble

through the hedgerows this morning?"
suggested Ralph.

"Oh, how lovely," said Mum. "The
twins would love that. And we can get to
know the area."

Jonny looked disappointed. "I was
thinking of showing Poppy the den I
made last year," he said.

"Well, I suppose Jonny and Poppy could
go exploring with Violet," suggested Rose.

Violet harrumphed.

"You'll never enjoy yourself if you don't
make more effort," Ralph told her firmly.
"You look after Poppy and Jonny this
morning, please. Take Jonny back to his
den, would you?"

"What happens if I don't?" muttered
Violet sulkily.

"Nothing," said Ralph. "But you will be
letting Jonny and Poppy down."

Violet sighed. "It's so unfair! I'll only do

it if I can sleep all day tomorrow . . ."

"We'll see."

Poppy smiled at Violet and saw a flicker of a smile in return – but then Violet seemed to remember that she didn't smile any more, and her face quickly turned stony once again.

It seemed as if Mum, Dad, the twins and the Blooms would never set off for their ramble. They kept saying they were ready, then turning back for something. Finally they disappeared across the meadow, following the line of a brambly hedgerow.

"Great," said Jonny. "Let's go and find the den – it was really cool. We spent ages on it. You coming, Vi?"

"Nah," said Violet. "I've got a signal on my phone, so I'm going to message a few friends."

"Well, is it OK if Poppy and I go?" asked Jonny.

"Yeah, s'pose so. As long as you're back before Mum and Dad, I don't mind. Peace and quiet – bliss!"

Poppy was disappointed. She really wanted to try and get to know Violet – surely she couldn't be grumpy *all* the time. But Poppy's urge to follow the fairies was stronger.

"Cool. Let's take some juice and bread and apples, so we can stay out a bit longer," suggested Jonny.

"Good idea," said Poppy.

They divided their snacks between two backpacks, put on their trainers,

fetched the camera and wandered
through the clearing, which seemed
to Poppy like the gateway to another
world.

Chapter 8

This time Jonny turned to the left. The woodland by the river really *did* seem enchanted, and Poppy heard soft singing noises, and once when she peeked through the trees at the river, she thought she saw a circle of tiny fairies dancing on the other side.

"Look, Jonny," she whispered. "Fairies on the river bank. See!"

"I don't see anything, Poppy. Maybe it was a couple of butterflies ..."

"No, they were definitely fairies – they were wearing dresses made from petals of the wild flowers in our meadow: rubies and diamonds and sapphires – just as I imagined," she said.

"OK, I believe you," said Jonny. "But I didn't see them. Now, where is this den – it must be nearby . . ."

Poppy could tell that Jonny didn't believe her, but she didn't like to say so. It was true what his mum said – if you didn't believe, you'd never see magic.

Poppy took out her camera in case the fairies reappeared. But they seemed to have vanished, so she turned to follow Jonny.

"I'm sure it's just round this bend," he said. But he soon saw that there was nothing there. "Oh, that's odd . . . It was here, I'm positive." Jonny looked very disappointed.

"Maybe somebody moved it," said
Poppy softly. "Things don't always stay
the same."

"Perhaps you're right. There was this
tree bough and we covered it with woven
twigs to make a hide . . ."

"Why don't we have a different
adventure this year?" suggested Poppy.
"Let's cross the golden stepping stones and
see what's on the other side."

"I'm a bit worried about crossing the

river. I've never done that before," said
Jonny. "I'm not allowed."

"Oh, come on," urged Poppy. "It'll be
fun, and it's not as if the river is deep . . ."

Jonny thought about it for a moment.
"Yeah, let's go then," he said.

Poppy led the way this time – she was
dying to see what was across the river.

They reached the stepping stones, which
glistened in the sun. Carefully, Poppy
placed her right foot on the first stepping

stone, then took a nervous leap to the second . . . and the third. She got to the other side with a final leap.

It felt different on this side of the river, as if anything was possible . . .

She checked on Jonny's progress: he was almost across the river, so she scrambled up the river bank. At the top, she looked in wonder at what lay before her.

It was quite different to the meadow – hilly, with crags and valleys and lots of secret places. "Hurry!" she called back over her shoulder. "It's really wonderful!"

She ran across the little mounds near the river bank. "I'm going to pretend I'm a fairy!" she declared. "Let's fly across the hills, shall we? I'm sure we can make a den here, or we might even find a secret cave!"

"I'm going to pretend that I'm a knight on a huge horse and I'm going to save a

fairy princess!" said Jonny as he caught up
with her.

"No!" said Poppy. "The fairy princess
is going to save the knight because she's
braver! She wasn't afraid crossing the
golden stepping stones!"

"I wasn't scared!" protested Jonny. "Well,
maybe just a bit . . ."

They ran on, laughing, carried by the wind, and Poppy almost felt as though she really was flying.

Jonny stopped to catch his breath, but Poppy ran on to the very top of the slope. She looked across to the other side of the valley below. And she couldn't believe what she saw . . .

Chapter 9

A white foal with long, spindly legs was standing on a grassy ledge across the valley. But it wasn't an ordinary white foal.

As the sun shone behind it, Poppy could see the silhouette of the pony's head. And she was quite sure that, right in the middle of its head, there was a horn.

"It can't be . . . a unicorn!" she cried. "Jonny, come here quickly!"

"What are you talking about now,

Poppy?" asked Jonny; he hadn't seen the
foal yet.

"Sssshhh," said Poppy. "Don't frighten it.
There's a unicorn across the ravine."

"Oh, Poppy, you know there are no
such things . . ." But when Jonny caught
up with her, he gasped.

"I knew there was magic on this side of
the river!" exclaimed Poppy.

"I can't believe it!" said Jonny. "But
Mum did say she'd heard of a unicorn
sighting!"

"I'm going to take a photograph –
otherwise no one will believe us!" said
Poppy.

As she studied the foal through the lens
of her camera, she realized that it was
trapped on the ledge. "It must have slipped
down," she cried. "I think it's stuck!"

"Yeah," agreed Jonny. "Poor thing! We
should go for help."

"But no one will believe us . . ." Poppy
crept to the edge of the ravine and leaned
out to get a good photo of the unicorn.
She inched forward.

"Stop, Poppy!" shouted Jonny.

At that moment the ground gave way,
and Poppy slipped and slid down among
the loose rocks to a ledge below.

"Oh, Poppy! Are you OK?" called
Jonny anxiously, peering down at her.

"Yes, I'm fine!" she called back. She was
quite a way below Jonny, and there was a
steep slope beneath her. Poppy gulped
and tried not to look down. The
valley floor seemed a very long
way below her.

"Oh no!" said Jonny.
"Make sure you don't
fall off the ledge!"

"I'm going to stay
very still," said
Poppy, trying
to keep calm.

"You go and get help! I just need my mum and dad!"

"Yes, I'll get help and come straight back. Don't panic! I'll be as quick as I can," said Jonny.

Poppy was terrified, but she looked directly across at the unicorn and remembered that the foal needed help too; she tried to be brave.

"Help is coming for us!" Poppy's voice echoed across the ravine.

The unicorn foal neighed softly back to her.

She could hardly believe that she was stranded opposite a unicorn in a ravine in Fairy Moon. *I did want an adventure!* she thought. *And now I've got one!*

Chapter 10

Jonny raced back towards the camp. His heart sank when he remembered that his sister was the only person around! *I just hope Violet knows what to do*, he said to himself.

He ran down the river bank, across the golden stepping stones, and along the path to the gap in the trees. Soon he was back at the campsite. He dashed over to the camper van and saw that Violet was lying on a sun lounger, flicking through a magazine.

"Violet!" he cried. "We need your help. Quickly! Poppy's in danger. She's fallen onto a ledge in a ravine and there's a unicorn foal in danger too."

It was a few moments before Violet could take in the news. She seemed to weigh up Jonny's expression – which was one of sheer panic – then sat bolt upright. "Where is Poppy? Stay calm, Jonny. Tell me everything," she said as she pulled on her trainers.

Jonny explained how they'd crossed the river.

"Jonny!" said Violet. "I thought you were just going to find that den from last year! What on earth have you been doing? You know you're not allowed across the river."

"We were looking for the den, but we couldn't find it, and Poppy wanted to see what was on the other side, and then

we saw this unicorn—"

"Jonny! You're really scaring me now!"
said Violet. "Stop talking nonsense. Please.
Honestly – unicorns!"

"No, it's all true," he insisted.

Violet didn't understand what had
happened, but she grabbed her phone so
she could call for help.

Soon, she and Jonny were scrambling

up the slope on the far side of the river, not saying a word, intent on finding Poppy. They raced up to the edge of the ravine. Violet gasped when she looked over the steep crag and saw Poppy on the narrow ledge. The drop below made her feel dizzy.

"Oh, Poppy, I'm so sorry that I haven't taken good care of you! I've already called the rescue services, and the adults will be here soon too!" she said.

"Do they know about the unicorn?" asked Poppy.

"Erm, yes, I've let them know that there's a foal that needs to be rescued too," said Violet.

"There's nothing we can do for now. Let's sing something! That will make the time pass!" suggested Jonny.

So they sang "Daisy, Daisy, Give Me Your Answer Do", then "Puff the Magic

Dragon", followed by "You Are My Sunshine".

As they sang, Poppy looked at the foal. *I'm sure it's happy that we're here*, she thought.

"You're being so brave, Poppy!" said Jonny. "You're amazing!"

After what seemed like just a few minutes, a helicopter appeared overhead.

"Oh, hurrah! Help is here!" said Violet. "Don't worry, Poppy. As long as you do what you're told, everything will be fine!"

Poppy called over to the foal, "You'll soon be safe too!"

Chapter 11

The helicopter landed a safe distance away, and a rescue team jumped out, racing over to Poppy.

"We'll soon get you up from there," said one man with a friendly face. He weighed up the situation. "One of us will jump down to join you. He'll lift you up and I'll take hold of you!"

Poppy gulped nervously. She'd never been so scared . . . what if the rescue went wrong? It was a long way down. She took a deep breath.

Before she could blink, one of the men was at her side, lifting her up towards his colleague.

"I've got her!" said the friendly-faced man.

And with a big lift, she was back on solid ground!

Poppy let out a little cry of relief.

"Phew — I have never been so frightened," said Violet, rushing over to hug Poppy.

Jonny hung back shyly, then decided he was going to hug her too. "It's so nice to have you back up here!" he said.

Just then, Mum and Dad and the Blooms arrived, looking very relieved to see that Poppy was safe.

"What's been going on?" asked Dad.

"Jonny and I went on an adventure and we found this unicorn foal, and—"

"Oh, Poppy!" said Mum, holding her close. "You and your adventures!"

The rescue team gave Poppy some hot chocolate and placed a cosy blanket round her shoulders, and suddenly she started to feel shivery with shock.

Everyone turned to watch the rescue of the unicorn. The foal was agitated and scared, but they managed to lift it to safety. As they did so, the owners of Fairy Moon turned up too.

The helicopter team brought the foal over towards them. Poppy stared at it and stroked its pretty face and silky ears. Two ears. But no horn.

She turned to Mum; Mum held her close. "It's actually a normal little white foal, darling . . ."

"A bit like I'm actually a normal little girl," whispered Poppy.

"Exactly," said Mum. "It doesn't mean you're not a magical princess too."

"It's actually *our* foal, love," said the man who owned the campsite. "We've been looking for it. We'd never have found it without you!"

"Ah — its mum must be the white mare who's been looking sad in the field!" Poppy said, suddenly realizing.

"Exactly right!" said the man, gently placing a halter on the foal and leading it back to the camp. "You shouldn't have

wandered up here, but I can't thank you enough for finding our foal!"

They all headed back towards the campsite, and when they approached the field, the foal broke away – and raced towards its mum. When the white mare saw her foal, she was ecstatic and they nuzzled each other, then charged joyously around the field at top speed.

"How brilliant that they're back together!" said Poppy.

"You were very brave, Poppy!" Violet told her.

"It's just that I love adventures," Poppy explained.

"You know what?" said Violet. "I've just realized that I do too!"

After a picnic lunch, Violet came to sit with Poppy. "When I was a bit younger," she said, "I saw fairies dancing on the other side of the river . . . and I crossed the golden stepping stones too."

"Really?" said Poppy. "So do you believe in fairies?"

"Of course I do," whispered Violet with a wink. "Just don't tell my mum!"

"OK," said Poppy. "Our secret!"

"I'll take you and Jonny to where the fairies dance if you like . . ."

"That would be great!" exclaimed Poppy. "Let's fly there!"

"Yes, let's!" Violet's smile lit up her whole face.

Later, Poppy went to check on the foal, which charged over to see her.

Poppy smiled. "Such a beautiful little unicorn foal," she murmured.

Chapter 12

The rest of the week at Fairy Moon was wonderful. They fished in the river, sketched butterflies in the meadow, rode the ponies and fed the chickens. One afternoon Poppy was lying amongst the wild flowers, thinking about her wonderful holiday adventures. She decided to write to Honey and tell her all about it.

Dear Honey

I miss you! I hope you're having a lovely adventure. We've had a brilliant time here at Fairy Moon. It's really magical - you would love it! There's a golden river and Jonny's mother, Rose, said that fairies dance on the banks. Don't mention this to anyone - but I saw the fairies! No one but you would believe me, but that doesn't matter, because I can picture them inside my head. They were dainty and pretty in their sweet petal dresses!

Can you believe what happened at the start of the week? I wanted to cross the river and Jonny said no, but I said we might as well, so we did. Ha, ha, you know what I'm like! Well, on the other side, I slid down the edge of a ravine and I had to be rescued by helicopter! AGAIN!!! But there was a little foal on the other side of the ravine. It might sound silly but I was sure it was a unicorn. It turned out that its long ears pointing forward had tricked me — they looked like a horn. But even just believing it WAS ☆ a unicorn for even a little while was so EXCITING!!!

I've kind of got to know Jonny's sister Violet a lot better — and you know how she's sometimes really quiet, like she's too cool to speak to us? Well, she's not REALLY like that at all. Funny, isn't it? The foal wasn't really a unicorn and Violet wasn't really a grump! Things are different from what they first seem...

I'm attaching a pic of the foal. I've got to go and make some fairy wings from some really big leaves I found by the river. See you soon!
Love you
Poppy x X x x x ♡ x ☆ x X

THE END

Turn over to read the first chapter
of another Princess Poppy story,
Fairytale Princess . . .

THE END

Turn over to read the first chapter
of another Princess Poppy story,
Fairytale Princess

Chapter One

Poppy thought that her teacher, Miss Mallow, was absolutely brilliant. She was so kind and she was always thinking up ways to make her lessons really interesting and fun. Poppy especially loved Monday mornings because every week they had what Miss Mallow called "circle time". This was when each and every one of the children was given an opportunity to share something that was special to them with the rest of the class. It was called "circle time" because Miss Mallow made them put their chairs in a big circle in the middle of the classroom so that they could all see everything that was being shown.

Poppy nearly always brought in something.

One Monday, she was especially pleased with what she had brought – it was one of her most treasured possessions and she couldn't wait to show it. When Miss Mallow announced that it was circle time, everyone moved their chairs into position and then she went round the class asking each child if they had anything to share. By the time she came to Poppy, Poppy was almost bursting with excitement! She reached into her school bag, pulled out her special item and held it up for everyone to see.

"I got this from my grandpa. It's a book of fairytales and Grandpa told me that it is over a hundred years old! It belonged to Grandpa's granny, who was my great-great-granny Mellow!"

"That is lovely!" exclaimed Miss Mallow. " A true piece of history. In fact, it might be useful today. You see, I have something to share with all of you too."

"Maybe she's getting married to Prince Charming!" whispered Poppy to her best friend, Honey. But that was not Miss Mallow's news.

"Children, as you know, builders are working on the school hall at the moment and it is due to be ready in eight weeks," began Miss Mallow. "The stage will be redesigned with new lighting and scenery, there will be new flooring, the roof is being fixed so there will be no more leaks, and we'll have some lovely new chairs and curtains. The Headmistress has invited a special guest to reopen the hall. However, I think we should do something to make the reopening even more special so I've decided that we will put on our very own musical show! What do you think?"

"Yeah!" chorused the whole class.

"Yes, Poppy, what is it?" asked Miss Mallow, noticing that Poppy's hand had gone up as soon as she'd told everyone about her plan.

"Um, who is the special guest? And which show are we going to do?"

"Well, I was actually just coming to both things," smiled Miss Mallow, thinking how impatient and inquisitive Poppy was. "The guest is Bryony Snow, editor of top fashion magazine – Buttons and Bows. We need to impress Ms Snow – if she likes the show she is going to do a feature on it in the magazine, but most importantly we must put on a fabulous event for everyone in the village who has helped us to raise so much money for the hall."

All the girls in the class interrupted Miss Mallow with a huge cheer – Buttons and Bows was their favourite magazine, even though it was for grown-ups.

"But what is the show?" called out Tom impatiently.

"Well," continued Miss Mallow, "I'm going

to write it myself but the words and songs will be based on a well-known story. You all know lots of stories so I thought it might be fun if you helped me to choose. You tell me your ideas and I'll write them on the board. Poppy's lovely storybook might give you some inspiration."

Every single child started calling out their favourites before Miss Mallow had even finished speaking – she could hardly keep up with them!

"Snow White and the Seven Dwarfs," called out one girl.

"Annie!" yelled another.

"Sleeping Beauty," suggested Lola, peering over to look in Poppy's book.

"Treasure Island!" shouted Charlie, to a loud cheer from the other boys.

"Little Red Riding Hood," said Helena.

"Cinderella!" cried Poppy, looking wistfully at the exquisite pictures in Great-Great-Granny Mellow's fairytale book.

"Yeah, Cinderella!" agreed several other girls. "We love Cinderella."

"Peter Pan!" yelled Ollie.

"Enough!" gasped Miss Mallow. "My wrist is quite numb. We've got plenty to choose from now. I suggest you all copy down this list and have a good think about it overnight. Then tomorrow we can put it to a vote. The story with the most votes is the show that we will do."

Snow White & the
Seven Dwarfs
Annie
Sleeping Beauty
Treasure Island
Little Red Riding
Hood
Cinderella
Peter Pan

At break, Poppy, Honey, Sweetpea, Mimosa and Abi formed a huddle in the playground – they were desperate to talk about the show.

"Which story are you going to vote for?" asked Poppy.

"Cinderella!" replied the other four girls in unison – each imagining themselves in a starring role and dressed as a fairytale princess.

Princess Poppy
A True Princess

Poppy is feeling very sorry for herself.
She is convinced that everyone likes her
best friend Honey more than they like
her and that they think she is prettier too!
Poor Poppy doesn't even believe that
she is a true princess any more!

Princess Poppy
Ballet Dreams

Poppy and Honey are thrilled when
Madame Angelwing starts extra ballet
classes. At first, Poppy loves them, but she
soon feels that ballet is taking over her life.
When Honey decides to stick with
the classes and no longer has any time
for her best friend, Poppy feels very sad.

Princess Poppy
The Fashion Princess

Poppy and Saffron are at New York Fashion
Week. They've got an action-packed
itinerary, including fashion shows and
a city tour. But when Poppy finds the
supermodel Tallulah Melage sobbing
in a corner, she realizes that there's
a darker side to all the glitz.

www.princesspoppy.com

Princess Poppy
Haunted Holiday

Poppy and Honey are going to France
to stay in an enormous castle and they
can't wait. It's the first time Poppy's
ever been abroad or stayed in a castle.
But as soon as they arrive,
strange things start happening . . .

Princess Poppy
Pony Club Princess

Poppy is taking part in a Pony Club
competition with her cousin Daisy. They've
both been practising like mad and they
absolutely can't wait. But before long
a whole series of things start to go
wrong and it looks like Poppy might
not be able to compete after all.

www.princesspoppy.com